Merry ?, 1990

Love,
Dad & Mom

the BETTER
BUTTER BATTLE

The mission of Wolgemuth & Hyatt, Publishers, Inc. is to publish and distribute books that lead individuals toward:

- A personal faith in the one true God: Father, Son, and Holy Spirit;

- A lifestyle of practical discipleship; and

- A worldview that is consistent with the historic, Christian faith.

Moreover, the company endeavors to accomplish this mission at a reasonable profit and in a manner which glorifies God and serves His Kingdom.

Illustrations by Vic Lockman.

Wolgemuth & Hyatt, Publishers, Inc.
1749 Mallory Lane, Suite 110, Brentwood, Tennessee 37027.

Library of Congress Catalog Number: 90-12291

the BETTER BUTTER BATTLE

by MARY PRIDE

Wolgemuth & Hyatt, Publishers, Inc.
Brentwood, Tennessee

One fine sunny morning
one year in the fall
I and my father went down to the Wall.
And he said to me,

"Son, what you see here today
will tell if the battle is going our way.
It's time that you knew of the Big Butter Battle.
For when you grow up,
you'll inherit my cattle.
And cattle are what
this here battle's about."

So I listened and watched
with my eyes bugging out.

I saw the big cannons!
I saw the big guns!
I saw all the soldiers!
And bombs by the tons!

And all of them pointing right over the Wall!
But each side did nothing.
Yes, nothing
at all.

And my dad asked me, "Son,
    why is it that we're sitting
        so close to our foes without ever hitting?
    And why do you think
        they're not shooting at all?"
But I gave him no answer
    that day on the Wall.

Then my dad sighed and said, "Son,
You know that we're Yooks.
And the other side's Yikks.
That's in history books.

"My son, long ago, Yooks and Yikks got along. But then long ago, my son, something went wrong.

"Long, long ago, when grand-dad was a sprat
    no taller than this, and no bigger than that,
There arose a fierce Yikk
    they called Ivan-the-Striving.
He didn't care beans about Yikk-Land surviving.
    Ivan wanted to rule!
    Ivan wanted to boss!
And he didn't much care if the Yikks took a loss.

"This is how Ivan took over Yikk-Land, my boy.
And believe me,
     to tell you
          does not give me joy.

"He threw out their butter and made them eat
    plastic!
He told them that plastic made food taste fantastic!
And since Ivan owned every bit of that plastic
    he didn't much care if it made people spastic.

"Plastic made the Yikks sick
And *so* sad in the tummy.
   They cried
      and they sighed
      and they said, 'It's not yummy!'

"So proud Ivan called for his Red Plastic Guards.
And they stood under windows and in people's
    yards.
And they said,
    'You'll eat plastic
        and here is your quota.
    One cupful a day,
        and you'll eat each iota.

" 'And if you don't eat it,
   we'll send you to Camp.
In Camp it is dirty
   and dingy
   and damp.

"'And you'll sneeze and you'll freeze
as you choke down your "butter."
And then you'll admit that there is
no other.'

"And in every school, my son, this was the rule—
Every Yikk had to learn
    to eat plastic
    in school.

"And none of the teachers had freedom to mention
that plastic was quite a new-fangled invention,
and people had always enjoyed eating butter.
They had to pretend that there was no other.

1+2=
PLASTIC

"While Ivan was sternly oppressing the Yikks
      a few of the Yikks had come up with new tricks.
They snuck out of Yikk-Land by tens and by dozens
with mothers
      and fathers
            and uncles
                  and cousins.
They settled in Yook-Land
      where butter was butter
      and no one pretended there was any other.

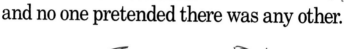

"My son," said my father, his hand on my head,
"Your grand-dad was part
        of that Yikk-crowd that fled.
He settled down here with his own herd of cattle.
And that was the start of the Big Butter Battle.
For Ivan-the-Striving was head of the Yikks.
But that wasn't enough for His Majesty's kicks.
He wanted to take over Yook-Land as well!
But here in free Yook-Land
        no plastic would sell.

"And, my son, we had cannons
     and soldiers
     and guns
     and Big Bomberoos by the thousands of tons.
We could have shot Ivan to small smithereens.
But Yooks weren't the type to be proud or be mean
     So we sat,
          and we watched,
          and let Ivan alone.
Perhaps we all figured he'd soon be dethroned.
After all, who with sense would prefer to eat plastic
     when butter is better, and tastes so fantastic?

"All our cheerleaders cheered for the Butter-Up Side,
And the Red Plastic Party was mocked and defied.
    But Ivan was smart.
    He knew just what to do.
    Ivan knew Ivan needed some cheerleaders, too.
Oh, he had his own cheerers, but they were a joke.
Ivan knew that he needed some help from *our* folk.

"He threw a big party!
He threw a big feast!
For cheerleaders both from the West and the East.
He showed them his factories full of red plastic,
And they all agreed that his scheme was fantastic.
      'The workers, so happy!
      The eaters, so merry!
      And look at their cheeks!
      They're as red as a cherry!
And every one does what you tell him to do!
Wish folks would all jump up when we whistled,
      too!'

"The cheerers went home
    with their heads all a-spinning.
And Ivan knew that
    soon his plan
    would be winning.

EAT PLASTIC

" 'Listen one, listen all!
    Who said butter is better?
    It's old-fashioned!
        Outmoded!
    Come, be a go-getter!
    Eat plastic! It's really much better for you!'

"Now the Yooks were confused.
      What to do?
      What to do?
'Our own cheerleaders say that Yikk plastic is best!'
Then your grand-dad stood up and said,

" "They've not confessed.
These cheerleaders yelling that plastic's a dream
Are living, I notice, on chocolate ice cream.
If they think plastic's great
        why don't they ever eat it?'

"The cheerers got nasty.
They said, 'Old man, beat it.
　　What do *you* know about issues of State?
　　Plastic is for the MASSES.
　　It's not for the GREAT!'

"When your old grand-dad saw
     he was getting nowhere
     he slowly came home and sat down in his chair.
And he said to me, 'Son,
     I have made a new rule.
     From now on,
        all you kids
           must not go to the school.

" 'For I fear that our cheerers
are teaching the lads
and the lasses
to scorn
all the ways of their dads.
Mark my words,' said your grand-dad,
'There'll soon come a day
when they'll take our own cows
and our butter
away.'

"Why, I thought the old man
        had become quite demented!
But for the moment
I was quite contented
        to play hookey,
        and watch the Yikks building the Wall
So big,
        and so high,
                and so thick,
                        and so tall.

'Ivan had died, to be followed by Wall-In.
Wall-In was worried his kingdom was fallin'.
So he grabbed all the land to the South and the West—
    Agraria
        and Check-Land
            and all of the rest.

"The Agrarians were brave.
They fought those old Yikks
        with mud
            and with stones
                and with rocks
                    and with sticks.
But the Yikks had big tanks.
And the Yikks had big guns.
And although we had Big Bomberoos by the tons—
        We didn't dare help them.
We sat on our fences
        and watched Yikks destroy the Agrarians' defenses.

"Then they hauled off our friends, and they
    put them on ice.
And we said, 'Naughty, naughty! That's not very
    nice!'
But the Yikks thumbed their noses—
Went on with their shooting—
    and trashing
    and smashing
        and burning
            and looting.
Before long, Agraria was behind the Yikks' Wall.
Your mother escaped just before the big fall.

"Well, your mom married me
       and we had our small farm.
As Yooks, for the moment we came to no harm.
But we saw the Wall grow
       around Check-Land and Pole-Land
       and Cue-Ball and Shawlistan,
       and round the Lowland.
In Bird-Land,
       the Wall traveled right through the city
       with barbed wire and guns and mines—
       not very pretty.
But still we Yooks sat on our side of the Wall
       with all our big guns, and did nothing at all.

"And your grand-dad was right.
For before long in school,
 the teachers were handing out
 Yikk-plastic gruel!
That horrible plastic made students feel cruel.
They fought with each other inside of the school.
But they all had to eat it—
 that was the rule.
And if any rebelled, they called him a fool.
And made him go sit on the Double-Think Stool.

"By now the cheerleaders were running the news.
They tried to get Yooks to put cows in the zoos.
They tried to make butter illegal, and they
Tried to get all the people a-thinking their way.
But Yooks kept on eating
        their butter
        on bread
        in spite of the cheerers and all that they said.
So the cheerers were frightened.
They thought, 'We might lose!'

"But then Yikk-Land developed some Big Bomberoos!

"Now the cheerers were happy.
They knew what to do.
    Make the people disheartened!
    Make all the Yooks blue!
Make them think they'd get blown up to Kalamazoo
    if they didn't get rid of their Big Bomberoo!

"So they told all the people,
    'It's *you* that's to blame
        for making the Yikks play this armament game.
The poor Yikks
    are so scared
    of our bombs
    that they just
Are helplessly driven to blow us to dust.'
And they told all the people
    'Now here's what you do . . .

"'Let's all put a freeze on the Big Bomberoo!
Let's put all our soldiers and armies on ice!
And make the Yikks promise that they will be nice!
We *know* we can trust them,
      for they are *good* Yikks
      and never,
      no, *never,*
            no, NEVER play tricks!'
And on the news night after night after night
Yook-Land always was wrong,
      and the Yikks,
      always right.

"Well, since that time, Son,
Yook-Land has been a-moping.
Because of the Bomberoos we've not been coping.
We won't fight a war—and, Son, if we get in it,
    we crawl away licked,
        and we won't try to win it.
That's how we lost Vet-Land and all of it neighbors
in spite of our soldiers and all of their labors.

"Though Wall-In is dead,
he was followed by Sneezer
And Boozer
    and Loser
        and Cough-Hack-and-Wheezer.
The Yikks are never too fond of these guys.
And they're sick of their plastic,
    which is no surprise.
So why do they keep putting up with it all?"

But I gave Dad no answer,
that day on the Wall.

I sat there and thought,
with my brain wildly spinning,
If butter is better,
      then why aren't we winning?
Then up strolled a chap with a mike in his hand,
      and a button that said,
         "Bomberoos Should Be Banned."
And he stuck his old mike right into my face
      and asked for *my* view of the Yook-Yikk arms race.

I felt my chest heaving!
I knew what to say!
I said, "Ban Bomberoos, sir?
    That is no way
    to solve all our troubles.
For Yikks have THEIR guns
    and Big Bomberoos by the thousands of tons.
We should *not* junk our guns,
    or arm soldiers with sticks.
We need our protection.
BUT NOT FROM THE YIKKS!

"Don't you see that the Yikks are just sick of their
    plastic?
The reason they fight us is 'cause they're all spastic.
But *who makes them eat it?*
Who wants *us* to try it?
I see your hand shaking!
But you can't deny it!

"The Bomb's not the issue.
The issue is Plastic.
For forcing it on us
       makes leaders bombastic!

"If you want to get rid of the Big Bomberoo
You'd better get rid of the Yikk-leaders, too.
    And here's how we'll do it.
    We'll stand by our butter!
    Why should we all tremble
        and mumble
        and mutter?
Get that Yikk-plastic back out of our schools!
Let the children go back to the Butter-Up Rules.
If you cheerers won't eat it,
    then why should we heed you?
Go live with the side
    that you'd rather have feed you!

"The Yikks *would* eat butter,
     if we would support 'em.
As for their leaders,
     they soon would export 'em.
Let's market our butter!
Let's all get aggressive!
Why should we support
     a regime
     that's oppressive?
Get rid of *those* guys, and you won't need a Wall.
When the Yikks are set free,
     then the Wall has to fall."

The voters all heard me speak live on the news.
And what do you think all those voters did choose?
Well . . .

Ten years ago I spoke up on the Wall.
And today on that spot
     is a big shopping mall
     where the Yooks and the Yikks
     both go shop for their butter.
And we all thank the Lord that there is no other!